PUFFIN BOOKS

MIND READER

Pete Johnson has been a film extra, a film critic for Radio 1, an English teacher and a journalist. However, his dream was always to be a writer.

When he was ten years old, he wrote a fan letter to Dodie Smith, author of *The Hundred and One Dalmatians*. She was to correspond with Pete for many years, and was the first to urge him to be a writer.

He has written many books for young readers and has 'proved himself time and time again to be an author of exceptional talents' – *The School Librarian*. His titles include, *The Cool Boffin*, *We The Haunted*, *Ten Hours To Live* and *The Vision*.

His most recent titles are, *The Ghost Dog*, which won the 1997 Stockton Children's Book of the Year, and the 1997 *Young Telegraph* Paperback of the Year, and *My Friend's a Werewolf*.

He has also written plays for the theatre and Radio 4. He is a popular visitor to schools and libraries.

Pete's hobbies include the cinema and pretending to keep fit.

SURFERS

MIND READER

Pete Johnson

Illustrated by
Ron Tiner

PUFFIN BOOKS

PUFFIN BOOKS

Published by the Penguin Group
Penguin Books Ltd, 27 Wrights Lane, London W8 5TZ, England
Penguin Putnam Inc., 375 Hudson Street, New York, New York 10014, USA
Penguin Books Australia Ltd, Ringwood, Victoria, Australia
Penguin Books Canada Ltd, 10 Alcorn Avenue, Toronto, Ontario, Canada M4V 3B2
Penguin Books (NZ) Ltd, 182–190 Wairau Road, Auckland 10, New Zealand

Penguin Books Ltd, Registered Offices: Harmondsworth, Middlesex, England

First published 1998
1 3 5 7 9 10 8 6 4 2

Filmset in Bembo

Made and printed in England by Clays Ltd, St Ives plc

British Library Cataloguing in Publication Data
A CIP catalogue record for this book is available from the British Library

ISBN 0–140–38814–1

Contents

Chapter One
The Dangerous Gift

FIRST OF ALL don't be scared of me. By myself I have no special powers at all.

My name is Matt, nickname Spud because my nose looks a bit like a potato.

I'm the most ordinary boy you'll

ever meet. Or I was until . . . now I'm jumping ahead. And I want to tell you everything, just as it happened.

It all started when I was left something in Mrs Jameson's will. I was totally amazed. I'd never been left anything in a will before.

Mrs Jameson was a very old lady. I first visited her with a harvest festival gift from our school.

She frowned at me. "None of it looks very fresh – and bananas give me indigestion, you know."

"Oh, sorry about that," I replied, not sure what else to say.

"Still, I suppose I could eat some of it. You'd better come in."

We sat in her kitchen. She poured me a glass of orange juice. Then I asked her if she liked living on her own.

"Yes of course I like it," she snapped. "Other people cause problems. You can't trust one of them." She glared at me. I hastily changed the subject.

Around her neck she was wearing a crystal. It caught my eye right away. She saw me looking at it.

"This crystal was left to me by my great aunt who took a shine to me. A strange woman; used to call herself a wizard. You didn't know there were any female wizards, did you?"

"No," I said. Actually I didn't know many male wizards either − not personally anyway.

She leaned forward. "This crystal is priceless. But no one else knows my crystal's true worth – and that's how it must stay. Otherwise I'd never have a moment's peace."

She was exaggerating now. She must be.

Still, I must admit the crystal fascinated me. Maybe because there were flashes of so many colours in it.

"I love all the colours you can see," I said, "especially that sky blue at the centre." Then I added hastily: "It is blue, isn't it?"

She looked puzzled by my question so I thought I'd better explain. "Only I'm what they call colour-deficient. I can see every single colour, I just see it in different ways. So I might see red as brown and brown as red. Blue and purple are pretty confusing too. That's why I asked."

"The crystal is blue in the centre, just as you said," she interrupted. Her eyes were blue too, and they were staring intently at me.

"Oh good, because sometimes I can make embarrassing mistakes. I went into a pet shop once and asked for the gold hamster."

For the first time she gave a wheezy laugh, then said slowly, "You just see in your own world of colour, that's all. I expect my crystal is more beautiful through your eyes than anyone else's." I really liked the way she said that. She made me feel special.

After that I visited her almost every day. We sat in her kitchen talking about practically everything. But then she became ill. She had pneumonia. She didn't want to leave her home but the doctor insisted. She'd only been in hospital for a couple of days when she died quite suddenly. She'd done that just to spite the doctor. That's what I told myself to try and cheer myself up.

I thought about her a lot over the next few days.

Then I discovered she'd left her precious crystal to me. She'd written me a letter too. On the envelope she'd put: "STRICTLY PRIVATE: FOR MATTHEW COLLINS ONLY." I'm not sure exactly why, but my hands shook as I opened the envelope.

Inside was her letter to me. Her handwriting was very shaky and difficult to read. Finally I made out: "Dear Matthew, I am leaving you my most valuable possession in gratitude for all those enjoyable hours we spent talking together. I do not want anyone else to discover how special my crystal is – ONLY YOU. But Matthew, you must keep the secret and you must be careful, because my gift can be VERY DANGEROUS as you will discover . . ."

This was followed by some squiggles which I couldn't read. The letter wasn't finished.

I stared and stared at it. What did Mrs Jameson mean about my crystal being very dangerous? That didn't make any sense. And what would I discover?

Then my mum peeked over my shoulder at the letter. "Poor thing," she said, "she was probably wandering in her mind when she wrote that. I expect she just wanted to make sure you took care of her gift."

But I didn't think that was true. Mrs Jameson's mind was sharp right to the end. She was trying to tell me something about the crystal, something very important.

But what?

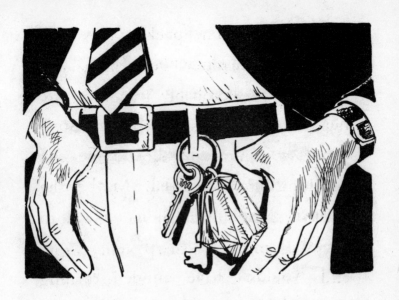

Chapter Two

Secrets of the Crystal

I PUT THE crystal on a keyring. I wore it to school on a loop on my belt. Even some of the teachers admired it.

After school the crystal sat on the telly in my bedroom. When the sun came down the crystal would shine all these different colours on to my wall: blue, pinkish red, green, yellow.

Then it did seem like a magic crystal. I thought of Mrs Jameson's great aunt, the wizard. Did she cast spells with this crystal? Maybe she turned people she didn't like into slugs.

I wouldn't have minded turning Craig Atkins into a slug. He was a new boy at our school who just loved himself. He was always boasting about his house and how he had a heated swimming pool and a pool table and . . . but I never listened to him.

I hated him. I especially hated the way he smiled – like a cat who's not only swallowed all his cream but all yours too.

Then, just messing about, I picked up my crystal and said, "Hocus pocus, make Craig Atkins into a slug."

I was only fooling around and really didn't expect anything to happen.

But something did.

The crystal started getting warmer. It was like when you put your hand on a radiator which has just been switched on. You can feel the heat stealing up your fingers, can't you?

Well, it was the same with my crystal. And then the crystal went on getting hotter, until in the end it seemed to be burning into my hands. I wasn't able to hold it any more. I let it drop on to my bed.

For a few seconds my fingers were still tingling. I couldn't believe how hot that crystal had become. I shivered with the shock.

I gave the crystal a quick prod. It was cold again. Yet as soon as I picked it up exactly the same thing happened: the crystal got warm, then after thirty-four seconds (I timed it) it became so hot I had to let it go.

But how weird.

I was tempted to run downstairs and tell Mum and Dad. But Alison, my older sister and my mortal enemy, was also downstairs and I didn't want her knowing about this. She'd already cast envious eyes on my crystal, saying how it was wasted on me.

And some words from Mrs Jameson's note rushed into my head: "You must keep the secret."

I'd never heard of a crystal which could get hot all by itself. That would certainly make it very valuable.

But Mrs Jameson hadn't just written "valuable". She'd put "very dangerous" as well.

I still didn't understand that. Then I suddenly thought: what if the crystal can put spells on people too? What if one second Craig is posing about by his pool and the next he's scuttling about as a slug.

I'd love to see his parents' faces when this slug starts chattering to them, claiming to be their marvellous son.

Of course I was only fooling about. Craig would be back at school tomorrow, wouldn't he?

Chapter Three
A Tremendous Discovery

FIRST OF ALL Craig wasn't at school. My hopes began to rise. I'd become quite keen on him turning into a slug.

But at breaktime there he was: an annoying grin plastered all over his face as usual. He was wearing his new designer-label green shirt; he looked like a long, processed pea in it. To make matters worse he was talking to Cally.

Despite what you may have heard, Cally is not exactly my girlfriend. She is more a mate. My best mate, to be exact.

Maybe you think that's a bit unusual. But she's been my best mate for more than two years now; since not long after she moved here, in fact. At first I'd see her at school and out walking Bess, her pet spaniel, but I never really spoke to her until the day Bess ran off. And I was the one who found her.

Cally was so relieved. Her parents were too – they invited me in for tea. I felt shy. I wasn't sure what to say. I noticed Cally was watching football on the telly so I said, "Oh, you like football, then, do you?"

"Thought I'd only like netball, did you?" she replied with heavy sarcasm. "Whenever a girl shows an interest in football why do all boys' chins hit the ground?"

"My chin's just fine," I replied. "I bet you know far more about football than me, anyway."

She did. Much more. But then she'd gone to her first football match – with her dad – when she was only four. At five she became her team's mascot.

"Who is your team now?" I asked.

"Spurs, of course," she smiled. "They're the only team worth supporting." She told me all about

Spurs, showed me her Spurs calendar, her Spurs torch, her four Spurs shirts.

She made it all sound quite exciting. That's when I thought I might as well support Spurs too. I'm still not such a mad fan as Cally, but I come quite close these days.

Her dad would sometimes take us to major Spurs games. It's so much better than watching it on the telly, for when you're there you're a part of it. Her dad was hoping to get tickets for the big Spurs versus Arsenal match. I was really looking forward to that.

Anyway, Cally and I go round together a lot and we get on really well. In fact, there's only one subject we disagree strongly about: Craig Atkins.

If Cally thought that he was an utter turnip-head – and she said she did – why was she always talking to him? Like now. I had a horrible feeling she was more impressed by him than she was letting on.

That's why I decided to tell her about my crystal. After all, my crystal was much more exciting than anything Craig could boast about. In fact, my crystal was probably the only one of its kind in the world.

I planned to tell Cally at lunchtime.

I stood waiting for her in the corner of the playground where we usually meet up.

I wanted to check the crystal was still working. I held it and nothing seemed to be happening. My heart sank. Maybe it only worked at night. Out of the corner of my eye I saw Craig walking towards me. He was the last person I wanted to talk to now. I deliberately looked away.

Then heat started to surge through again. I let out a great sigh of relief. In the back of my head I could hear Mrs Jameson whisper: "You must keep the secret." I felt a stab of guilt. But I would swear Cally to secrecy and I wouldn't tell anyone else. Not ever.

Then I heard another voice whisper: "Great that Cally's dad has got some tickets for the Spurs versus Arsenal match! I bet she takes me not Spud this time. He's so boring."

I recognized the voice instantly. It was Craig. I jumped around, thinking he was right behind me, that was how close he sounded. But in fact he was still a couple of metres away from me.

I let go of the crystal.

He grinned at me. "Waiting for Cally, are you?" He said this so casually I could only stutter, "Yes." Then he gave me this big, friendly wave and he was gone.

I stared after him. I couldn't believe the way he'd blurted all that out to me then acted so cool. He must be very sure of himself.

And why had Cally told him about her dad having the tickets rather than me?

I was very uneasy. And for the moment I forgot all about my crystal.

I let Cally know what Craig had

said. She was totally amazed. "I just happened to mention to him that my dad had got the tickets, that's all. I was going to tell you too."

"Were you?"

"Of course I was," she laughed. "I only told him because he was showing off as usual and I wanted to shut him up."

"I see." I laughed as well, half-reassured.

After school we confronted Craig together. He played a blinder. He denied saying anything to me about Cally's football tickets. He claimed they were the last thing on his mind.

He gave quite a performance. I must admit that. He even swore on his life that he hadn't said anything to me.

Still, he could deny it as often as he liked. I'd heard him.

On the way home (Cally's house is on the way to mine) I said to her, "Craig's trying to cover up now by pretending he didn't say anything about your tickets. Still, you know Craig, his face would explode if he told the truth."

Cally laughed and nodded in agreement. She said, "Everyone's been asking me about the Spurs–Arsenal match. My dad was so lucky to get tickets. People keep coming up to me saying what big Spurs fans they are, and can they come with me."

I stiffened.

"Perhaps", she went on, "I should put all their names into a hat, or maybe

22

I should have a quiz about Spurs and let the biggest fan come. What do you think?"

I was too hurt to reply. What was she playing at? I was her best mate, therefore I should go with her. End of story. I decided having these tickets had really gone to her head.

Well, I'd show her I didn't care. I still had my amazing crystal. Cally was going to get a shock in a moment.

But it wasn't her who got the shock – it was me.

For I suddenly heard her whisper: "Craig sounded as if he was telling the truth. Did Matt make all that up about the tickets just to turn me against Craig? I don't like that."

I was stunned, not just by what Cally

was saying but the way she was speaking, as if I wasn't there. Was she trying to be funny?

I turned to argue with her. She was still babbling away about how I didn't own her but her lips weren't moving.

HER LIPS WEREN'T MOVING.

In fact, her whole face was completely still.

What was going on here?

The hairs rose along the back of my head.

This was so weird. It was as if Cally's voice had somehow escaped from her body. And I could hear it so clearly. It sounded as if she was whispering something very confidentially in my ear.

Only she wasn't.

Really, she was deep in thought, completely unaware that I could hear her.

The crystal was becoming very hot now. I had to let it go. At once Cally's voice sprang back into her body again.

I gaped at her in amazement. My heart was beating furiously.

"What's the matter?" asked Cally. This time her lips were moving again.

"The matter?" I stuttered.

"You look like you've just seen a ghost . . . Are you all right?"

"No, I feel a bit sick, that's all." And actually my stomach was like jelly. "So I won't stop off at your house this evening, I'll go straight back."

"Yeah, sure. But will you be all right?"

I nodded. "Say hello to Bess for me – and Craig really did say all that stuff, you know. You've got to believe me."

"Don't be silly. Of course I believe you," said Cally.

I stumbled off.

"Matt."

I turned round. Cally gave me a little smile. "No, I'll tell you later," she said.

I walked a few metres, but my legs felt like lead. Then I stopped. What had just happened didn't make any sense. People only spoke without moving their lips in films that hadn't been dubbed properly.

Either I was going mad or I had just made the most tremendous discovery about my crystal.

Chapter Four
Testing the Crystal

I STARED DOWN at the crystal. I hardly
dared breathe on it.

Now I know what Mrs Jameson
meant: it was priceless. For this crystal
would let me peer into people's minds.
I could discover the most top-secret

information.

Actually, I already had.

Craig didn't say a word about the Spurs tickets. He only thought it and I "overheard" him. No wonder he was so indignant.

Still, it served him right for even thinking it. And at least I knew what Craig was up to.

"I have the power to read minds." I kept muttering this over and over to myself, just as if I were casting a spell.

I still couldn't take it in.

I had to test out the crystal again. This time I decided to try it on a complete stranger.

But who?

People were walking past so quickly and I couldn't start trailing after one of them. They'd get suspicious. Then I stopped at the sweet shop. The couple who owned the shop were away. I didn't know the woman who was standing in for them.

I went inside the shop.

"Hello," I said, smiling cheerily at the woman.

She just gave me a frosty glare in reply.

I told her what I wanted, then I pointed my crystal towards her. The crystal grew warmer. She was weighing up my sweets. She didn't look up. But all at once I overheard: "Shall I wear my blue hat or my red one to the wedding? The blue hat matches my jacket but the red one is more expensive."

She handed me the sweets. I gave her the exact money, then said, gravely, "I should wear the blue hat if I were you." She looked so shocked I thought her head was going to start spinning.

"How do you know that?" she gasped at last.

"Don't worry, I know everything," I replied. "Do enjoy your wedding, won't you. Goodbye for now."

She didn't answer, just put out a hand as if to stop herself from falling.

Outside the shop I laughed and laughed. The look on her face — I'll never forget that.

What a brilliant crack! It was only afterwards I wondered if I'd been a bit . . . well, reckless. For I'd drawn attention to myself. That woman could tell her friends. Gossip could start.

I decided I had to be more careful, more discreet.

For if anyone ever found out about my crystal . . . well, the world would be at my door, wouldn't it? I'd never have a moment's peace. I certainly would never dare wear my crystal in case someone tried to steal it. I'd probably have to keep it in a vault.

Plus if the government ever found out about it, they'd want to perform tests on it.

And only one person was going to do tests on this crystal – me.

Chapter Five
Talking to the Dead

NEXT DAY I bought a notebook so that I could jot down everything I discovered about my crystal. Only I decided it was too risky to refer to the crystal directly, especially if my notebook got into the wrong hands (for example, my sister's).

So I gave my crystal a code name. I called it "The Third Ear".

And then I jotted down all I'd discovered about my "third ear". Some amazing things, actually.

For instance, if I wanted to know what someone was thinking I just pointed my crystal in their direction. And it didn't matter how far away they were.

I discovered that when I was playing football. I'm not really good at football. I just like playing it, even if I usually end up in goal. I was in goal, that day. We were playing Wycliffe, the school down the road from us and our big rivals.

I let in two goals but also made a

couple of pretty good saves. So it was two-all when right at the end of the match came a penalty.

Talk about pressure: everyone was calling out things to me. But I was only listening to one person. (The crystal was tucked safely in my pocket.) He was a few metres away from me. But when I tipped the crystal towards him I picked up: "I'll let their goalie think I'm going for the left corner and then do the opposite."

Of course I dived to the right and made the most magnificent save, even if I say so myself. My team went crazy. Someone even called me the supreme penalty saver.

And I just lapped it up.

Now what else could my crystal do?

Well, it travelled through glass. I could stand by the kitchen window and pick up what my mum was thinking in the garden (very boring it was too). But it couldn't travel through walls (tried this a couple of times) and it didn't work on the telephone or with the television.

What about with animals? It would be great if the crystal was able to pick up their thoughts. I decided to test it out on the cleverest dog I know – Bess. She's incredibly obedient. It's no wonder she's won so many prizes and looks certain to win lots more.

My moment came after school. I was round Cally's house. She went inside to get us some drinks. I was left in the garden with Bess. I called her over. She came at once.

And when she saw the crystal she pricked up her ears and seemed really excited. But all I picked up was this strange, whooshing noise, just like when you hold a shell up to your ear.

Later when Bess was asleep she started whining and shaking her legs. She was dreaming. I've always wanted to know what dogs dream about. I nudged the crystal towards her but all I got was that whooshing noise again.

It seemed the crystal only worked on humans. Then I had a crazy thought: might the crystal work on dead bodies as well as live ones?

I'd always wanted to know if we could contact the dead.

Maybe I was about to find out. I

might discover what happens after you die.

Shudders ran through me.

This was getting creepy – but fascinating.

I decided to test out my theory at the local cemetery. I went there in the early evening. I wanted it to be dark – but not too dark. I slumped down by a grave. My hand was shaking. The crystal started to get warm, then this croaky old voice began whispering in my ear.

"Are you all right?" he asked.

"I'm fine," I spluttered. "How about you?" Then I realized that was a stupid question, for if he was all right he wouldn't be where he was.

"I mean, what's it like . . . there?"

"What's it like?" he repeated. That's when I realized that not only could I hear a dead man — I could feel his breath on my ear.

I whirled round and nearly cannoned into this old man. We stood gaping at each other.

"Are you sure you're all right, lad?" he quavered, at last.

Very embarrassed now, I stuttered, "Oh yes. It's just I thought you were someone else. Bye."

I ran all the way home.

Later I wondered if I should repeat the experiment. But I wasn't eager to return to that graveyard. Not on my own, anyway. Instead, I decided to test my crystal on one of the living dead — Mr Rickets, the history teacher!

Chapter Six
Amazing, Sensational News

EVERYONE MESSES ABOUT in Mr Rickets' class. It's sort of compulsory.

We used to have these great ink fights in his class. I'd go home with my shirt absolutely covered. Trust parents to ruin the fun by complaining. Now teachers – and sometimes the headmaster – patrol around outside Mr Rickets' class. They pretend they're not but at the slightest sign of any trouble one of them always pops in.

Mr Rickets was talking about Henry VIII that day, I think. I couldn't be sure as everything he says goes through my head and falls out on the other side.

I directed the crystal towards him and tuned in. This really whiny voice came through, moaning about how he could never engage this class's interest even though he had tried so hard. Now all he had to look forward to was his cup of coffee at breaktime.

It was quite sad really. The crystal was becoming hot and I was about to tune out when I heard: "So tired and my wig's so itchy again."

His wig?

Hold the front page! Rickets wears a wig.

This was amazing, sensational news. For while we had often commented on the awfulness of Rickets' hair – it was all permed and feathery – no one had guessed that it wasn't his own.

I was so excited I whispered the news to Cally at once. Of course I couldn't say I'd "overheard" Rickets, so instead I claimed I'd seen the join at the back of his head.

That news went round our classroom like wildfire. Soon everyone was studying Rickets with more attention than they'd ever given him before. Rickets even gave us a small smile. He must have thought he'd suddenly become interesting.

He set us some work. We all piled up to his desk to ask him stupid questions, while scrutinizing the back of his head. Then Andy Grey gave me the thumbs up – he'd spotted the join too.

I'd been proved right. Pleased by my discovery, I was eager to find out more about the wig. So at the end of the lesson I stood asking Mr Rickets about homework, while activating my crystal. I didn't pick up anything more about the wig – but I discovered there was going to be a surprise test on Henry VIII tomorrow.

Usually Rickets' surprise tests caught me out. But not this time.

On the way home I tuned into Cally. She still hadn't offered me the other ticket for the Spurs versus Arsenal match. I was anxious because of Craig. He was still hanging around with Cally. Today I had heard him boasting to her about all his computer games and CDs. Was he impressing her?

But she wasn't thinking about Craig. She was worrying about her school work. Her parents thought she should be getting higher marks. They'd been nagging her about that. And she really didn't want to let her parents down. But she was doing her best. Why couldn't they see that?

I felt very sorry for Cally. That's why I blurted out: "I've got a feeling there might be a test on Henry VIII tomorrow."

She looked puzzled. "Rickets never said anything."

"Oh, you know how he loves to give us surprise tests. There'll be a test tomorrow. You'll see."

Sure enough, next day there was a test on Henry VIII. By the following lesson Rickets had marked the test, and guess who got top marks ... Well, in fact Cally did. She got three more marks than me. I came second. But that was cool because Cally was so happy.

The day was spoilt though by someone (I'm sure it was Craig) scrawling on the board: RICKETS WEARS A WIG. Underneath he'd drawn this cartoon of a bald man. (A two-year-old could have drawn something better.)

And Rickets saw it. We expected him to explode, put the whole class in detention. Instead, he just picked up the board rubber and erased the offending picture.

He didn't say a word. But his eyes seemed to have closed up. And I knew – without needing to consult the crystal – that he was feeling sick inside.

He had massive problems keeping classes in order anyway. Now, thanks to me, he had a fresh one – because of course the whole school knew about his wig by now.

I felt more than a bit sick too. I'm

sure I wasn't using the crystal as Mrs Jameson intended. I was acting just like a pickpocket, foraging around in people's heads and stealing their secrets. You've heard of peeping Toms. I was the first listening Tom.

But later I changed my mind. After all, if I had supersonic hearing you wouldn't expect me to plug up my ears every time I went out, would you?

So what's the difference with my crystal?

I did make this pledge, though. Everything I found out by 'tuning-in' would remain in confidence, save for anything which might do me or my friends harm.

That was fair, wasn't it?

From now on I was determined to

use my crystal properly and not make any more mistakes.

But I did – an even worse one too.

Chapter Seven
End Of a Friendship

ON SATURDAY MORNING I went to the Spring Fair at our school with Cally. I had to lend her five pounds as her parents never give her much pocket money, but I didn't mind. Craig was prowling around there too.

On one of the stalls was the biggest jar of sweets I'd ever seen. It was enormous. You could win all those sweets if you guessed how many were in the jar. People kept asking the man in charge of the stall to give them a clue. Every time he smiled but refused. Then Craig announced he knew how many sweets were in the jar.

If Craig won the sweets he'd go on about it for weeks . . . centuries. It would be yet another trophy for him to show off to Cally about.

I had no choice but to enter the competition too. Luckily my crystal had "overheard" the organizer. I knew exactly how many sweets were in the jar.

And so I won it.

I strolled triumphantly around the fair with my jar of sweets – remarkably heavy it was too. A little voice inside my head wondered if I'd cheated. But I swept the voice away by pointing out that if I hadn't butted in Craig would have certainly won, as his guess was the nearest after mine. So actually I'd saved the world from a very tragic event.

Also, I shared my sweets around which was more than Craig would have done.

Cally was dead impressed. "But you guessed it exactly right. How did you do that?"

"I'm a genius."

She laughed.

"And I had inside information."

She laughed again.

"No, I was just lucky, I suppose," I said finally.

"You've been very lucky recently, haven't you?" said Cally. "And perhaps you'll go on being lucky," she added, with a teasing smile. She wouldn't say any more. But I took that to mean she was going to let me have the other Spurs ticket.

And about time too. I was her best friend and I had helped her get top marks in the History test. I deserved that ticket.

But on Monday I received a big shock. I was sitting in a lesson, with the jar of sweets beside me. I still had hundreds left. And I was just casually tuning into a few people, or surfing as

I call it. It wasn't very exciting – most of them were just thinking about food – but then I directed my crystal at Craig.

To be honest, I didn't enjoy tuning into him. I hated to hear his voice whispering in my ear. Yuk! But I had to know what the enemy was thinking.

Craig must have noticed me glancing at him because I "overheard": "I'd love to tell Spud, but Cally's sworn me to secrecy. Shame. Because if he knew Cally was coming round my house tonight . . ." Then he started to laugh in his head. Horrible braying sounds which instantly gave me a migraine.

All day I walked around in a fog of misery. I didn't get a chance to say anything to Cally until we were walking home together.

I told myself to be calm, be cunning. So I asked as lightly as I could manage: "What are you doing this evening, then?"

Cally shrugged her shoulders. "Nothing much, just do my homework and wash my hair, the usual." Then she changed the subject.

Of course I knew she was lying. It was becoming harder to control my anger. "I see Craig's still creeping around you just so you'll give him the Spurs ticket."

Cally's face reddened.

"He's got a nerve, hasn't he, trying to steal my ticket?" I went on.

"Your ticket!" she exclaimed.

"Yes, you're going to give the other ticket to me, aren't you?"

Cally didn't say anything, just gave a strange kind of half-laugh. Was she amused? Was she starting to feel guilty?

My crystal would know.

This is what it picked up . . . "Just sick of Matt going on about this Spurs ticket all the time like it's his property. Well, I'll show him. When I go round to Craig's house tonight, I'll see if he wants the ticket."

I snatched my hand away from the crystal. I felt as if I'd just been punched in the stomach. I hardly spoke to Cally after that – and she hardly spoke to me either.

All evening my head was in a whirl. I wanted to go to Craig's house –

sorry, mansion – and smash all his windows. I wanted to do something bold and dramatic and nasty. I plotted all sorts of impossible things in my head.

I hardly slept that night.

Next morning I arrived at school to see Cally and Craig laughing together in the playground. Something in me just snapped. I stormed over to Cally. "I hope you and Craig enjoy the football match together," I sneered. "And I want the five pounds I lent you on Saturday. I'm always lending you money and not getting it back." I was practically shouting now. People were gathering round. But before Cally could reply I'd shot away again.

She didn't sit with me in

registration. Well, I didn't care. But at breaktime she was waiting for me by my locker.

She hissed, "I wouldn't go to a Spurs match with Craig if you paid me. You don't know me at all, do you?" Then she thrust an envelope in my hand before walking off. I ripped the envelope open. Inside were five one-pound coins and a note: "Here's the money I owe you. I HOPE YOU CAN BUY YOURSELF A NEW ATTITUDE WITH IT."

She'd pressed down so hard with her pen there were little tears on the paper. The words seemed to jump up and hit me in the face. I blinked furiously.

I'd over-reacted, hadn't I? Just because you think something, doesn't mean you're going to do it. In the heat of the moment you can think all sorts of wild things.

Cally had no intention of really giving Craig the Spurs ticket. I should have realized that. I'd acted foolishly. I'd acted without thinking. But these days I never seemed to have the time to hear my own thoughts. I was too busy listening in to everyone else.

I tried to patch things up with Cally. But every time she blanked me out. The following Monday I heard her talking about the Spurs versus Arsenal match. She'd gone with her cousin, Giles, who I knew she didn't even like much. I blocked up my ears and walked away.

Soon she and I got into the habit of

not talking. That wouldn't have mattered if I didn't miss her so much.

I especially hated walking home from school on my own. But I still had my trusty crystal. I went surfing: it was good fun tuning into complete strangers. Even if most of their thoughts were dull or made no sense.

One day, I thought, I'll do this and tune into something really bad.

And that's exactly what happened.

Chapter Eight
A Terrible Discovery

IT WAS FRIDAY afternoon. I was trailing home. I'd tuned into this woman who was singing to herself – a soul number which I'd never heard before – quite unaware that her song was flittering around in my head too.

59

But even that didn't cheer me up. All day long my head was full of voices and I had never felt so lonely.

Then I passed Cally's house. Cally had been away ill from school for the past two days. I stopped, hoping to catch a glimpse of her. Maybe we could talk more easily out of school. I wanted this silly feud between us to stop.

I didn't see Cally but I spotted Bess asleep in their porch. She saw me and started barking and wagging her tail. She was still my friend.

"All right, quiet now, Bess," I called. She heard me and obeyed right away. She was such a great dog.

Then I spotted this guy on the opposite side of the road. And I had the weirdest feeling that he was watching me. So I tilted the crystal towards him. He murmured in my ear: "The family's away tomorrow so I'll grab the dog tomorrow evening. Yes, it's very quiet round here, so it should be easy."

Then I had to let go of the crystal. By the time it had cooled down the man was already walking away. I had to follow him, discover more.

I ran up to the top of the road. There was no sign of him. He'd vanished without trace. Maybe his car had been parked close by.

I immediately jotted down a description of him: quite old, completely bald, grey suit and wearing glasses the size of a small television screen. Not the sort of person I'd imagine stealing dogs. But then I supposed dog-nappers came in all shapes and sizes.

Certainly there'd been a piece in the local paper about this gang who went around stealing dogs, then demanded a ransom for them.

A shiver ran up my spine. Was this about to happen to Bess? I had to do something. But what? My head was spinning.

I went home. Eating my meal in a kind of trance, I decided I had to warn Cally. I rang her up. To my surprise she answered. I immediately put the phone down. It seemed such a crazy thing to tell her. Hello, your dog is going to be stolen tomorrow. Don't ask me how I know. I just do.

Then I had a better idea. I'd send Cally an anonymous note.

I wrote:

BEWARE, AN ATTEMPT WILL BE MADE TO STEAL YOUR DOG, BESS, TOMORROW. DO NOT LET YOUR DOG OUT OF YOUR SIGHT. GOOD LUCK.

A WELL-WISHER.

I slipped out, popped the anonymous letter through her letter box and raced home again.

I'd just got in when the phone rang. It was Cally. She was not happy. "Did you send me this stupid note?"

"Me?" I quavered.

"It was you, wasn't it?" she said. "You tried to disguise your handwriting, but I recognized it right off. And it was you who rang me, then put the phone down again. I checked."

"Well, you see . . ." I began.

But Cally went on. "You're trying to get back at me with these stupid little pranks that aren't even funny. I mean, my mum's worked up enough with all this in the local paper about dog-nappers, without you making things up."

"I'm not making it up," I said. "I'm trying to warn you to keep an eye on Bess tomorrow."

"You know we're going away tomorrow."

"You are?"

"We're going to a wedding. I told you about that weeks ago."

She had, as it happens. But I'd

completely forgotten. "So what are you doing with Bess?" I asked.

"Miss West, our next-door neighbour, is looking after her. And she used to breed dogs, so she knows how to care for them."

I pictured Miss West in my head. She hadn't lived there long and the first time I saw her I thought she had purple hair. Actually her hair was blue, although that was nearly as odd – to me anyhow. But she was a nice woman, smiley and friendly. She was pretty old, though.

"Bess could be snatched quite easily from Miss West," I cried. "I reckon that's why they've picked tomorrow."

Cally sounded both puzzled and exasperated. "Why are you doing all this? Is it because I didn't give you my Spurs ticket?"

"No, no," I practically shouted. "I couldn't care less about the Spurs ticket. I'm just trying to warn you about something very serious. Honestly."

There was a slight pause.

"But how do you know all this?" asked Cally.

"I overheard some people talking in the road."

"What people?"

"Er . . . two people. Two men."

"And what did they say?"

A long breath. "They said, 'There's a dog in that house and we're going to steal it tomorrow night.'"

"Well, they don't sound very good

criminals if they discuss their plans in the road for everyone to hear. I don't think we've anything to fear from *them*."

There was no disguising the sarcasm in Cally's voice. "And tell me, did these two men carry a bag marked 'Swag' and did they –"

'Look, I wouldn't make up anything bad about Bess. You must know that," I interrupted. For one mad moment I wondered if I should tell Cally about the crystal. But there was no time. She'd already rung off.

I thought of ringing Cally back. But I didn't know how I could make my story sound more convincing. Then I wondered about calling her mum. She was a tense, nervous woman – in fact

Cally had told me, in strictest confidence, that her mum had been on tranquillizers for a while. What if, after speaking to me, she became so anxious she started taking tranquillizers again.

And maybe I'd misunderstood that bald-headed man. I'd only caught a snatch of his thoughts. And he really didn't look like someone who belonged to a gang of dog-snatchers.

I paced around my room. Then I heard the sound of laughter downstairs. I went down and discovered my parents and Alison, my sister, playing cards.

Alison is usually out with Tony, her boyfriend. But tonight she was staying in (although Tony didn't know that) as she didn't want Tony to take her for granted.

"Let him wonder where I am," she said. "Let him worry a little."

My sister's cracked.

But I joined in the game of cards just for something to do really. My dad was in one of his silly moods and kept trying to sneak glances at our cards. Of course I didn't need to look at the cards. I just set my crystal to work, then I'd "hear" them pondering about the cards they had and what they should do next.

I won every game.

"What's your secret, Matt?" asked Mum.

"I'm just a very skilful person, I suppose," I said. My sister made throwing-up noises.

"Well, let's have one last game," said Mum, "and see if we can dethrone the champion."

It was going really well until I came to my sister. I turned to her and then discovered she was thinking in French. I struggled to understand, concentrating hard.

"Can't understand my French, can you?" she murmured.

"It's your rotten accent," I began.

Then I stopped and gazed at her in horror.

She gave me a triumphant smile in return.

My heart started to thump furiously.

"Come on, you two," said Dad. "Stop looking at each other and get on with the game." I was so thrown by what had just happened that I lost the game.

"Seems like your luck has finally run out," Dad said to me.

My sister was waiting upstairs for me. "You're either an alien, which wouldn't surprise me," she said, "or you're using that crystal to read minds."

"What are you talking about?" I gasped.

"I watched you," she said. "Every time you fiddled with that crystal you picked up what cards we had. And then when I started thinking in French you knew, didn't you? You knew."

"Don't be silly," I said.

"I'm not being silly," she snapped.

"Yes you are."

"OK. Well, I'm going to tell Mum and Dad, tell everyone." She was yelling.

"Keep your voice down."

"Why should I?" She had this really crafty smile on her face now. In the end, the only way I could quieten her down was to let her "have a go" with my crystal.

"Let me see if I can pick up your thoughts." She held the crystal just as she had seen me do.

Then I had an idea. I'd seen a film once about these alien children who could read minds. Only, the doctor stopped them reading his thoughts by building this wall in his head.

I had to do that. Then Alison would believe my crystal couldn't do anything. And my secret would be safe.

I imagined a great, high brick wall. I pictured the wall growing higher and higher. No one could ever see over the top of it. It hid everything . . . everything.

Suddenly my sister let out a cry. "Ow, that crystal gets hot, doesn't it?"

"Yeah, it does that sometimes." Then as casually as I could, "Hear anything, did you?"

"Yes," she said.

My heart started to thump.

"I heard this strange noise like when you put a shell up to your ear."

This was the same noise I'd heard when I tried to tune into Bess. But she hadn't picked up anything else. And she seemed to lose interest in my crystal after that.

My plan had worked. Still, it had been a close shave. And all because I had to show off when I was playing cards.

I shook my head. Mrs Jameson kept the crystal's secret all her life. I nearly gave away its secret in three weeks – and to my sister, of all people.

I read Mrs Jameson's letter again. If only she'd finished it instead of putting those daft squiggles. I needed to hear her words of wisdom about the crystal. I had a feeling I hadn't used it very wisely.

I lay awake for ages thinking about Bess. I still wasn't sure what to do. I couldn't call the police, because where was my evidence? Maybe Miss West would let me look after Bess tomorrow. That was an idea. Then at least I'd know Bess was safe.

I finally fell asleep. Next morning I woke up with a start. I sensed something was wrong.

I reached out for my crystal. I always keep it on the little table by my bed.

But it wasn't there.

Chapter Nine
The Missing Sister

I SHOT UP in bed and searched frantically for the crystal. It was gone – stolen.

I knew who the chief suspect was.

I ran into my sister's bedroom. Normally she lolled in bed until midday on a Saturday. But not today. I tore downstairs.

"I don't believe it. Another one up early," said Dad.

"There'll be pigs flying past the window next," said Mum. They were both sitting at the kitchen table reading the papers.

I burst over to them. "Alison. Where did she go?"

"Into town I suppose," said Dad. "I told her a lot of the shops wouldn't even be open yet, but she just shot out of the door."

"You should have stopped her," I shouted, "because she's stolen my crystal."

Both Mum and Dad gave me shocked looks.

"Alison wouldn't do that," said Mum.

'She's done it," I replied.

"You go upstairs and search properly before you start making accusations like that," said Dad.

But I just knew Alison had my crystal. I thought I'd cleverly put her off the scent last night. She'd been the clever one pretending to believe me, then sneaking into my room and nicking my precious crystal.

What was she doing with it now – testing it out on someone? Or maybe she was about to sell it? I wouldn't put anything past my sister.

I raced into town after her. It was still early, only about half past nine. And there weren't many people about. I should find my sister easily.

She was often hanging about in the town centre by the fountain.

But today she wasn't.

I saw other people I knew and normally I would have chatted with them. But today I just rushed past. I saw everyone except my sister.

She'd vanished.

She must be somewhere.

Think. Think.

She might have gone to Tony's home. Maybe she was going to try the crystal out on him.

I sped round to Tony's house. He lived near Cally. And on the way I saw Miss West. She was taking Bess for a walk. Bess yelped excitedly when she saw me. But Miss West didn't look very sturdy at all. Anyone could steal

Bess away from her. She recognized me.

"I'll take Bess for a walk later if you want," I said.

'That's kind of you, dear," she said. "But to be honest, I enjoy the exercise."

"Well, er, actually I could look after her all day if you like." My mum wasn't keen on dogs but she couldn't mind just this once.

Miss West gave me a strange look. "I'm sure we'll be fine," she said firmly. I think I'd offended her. She walked away with her head raised in the air. I'll just have to keep coming back and checking on Bess.

Then I reached Tony's house. He opened the door. He gazed at me hopefully. "You've got a message from Alison?" he asked at once.

"No."

His face fell.

"But she was here this morning?" I asked.

"Oh yes."

"And was she holding a keyring – with a crystal?"

He looked surprised by the question. 'That's right. I'd never seen it before."

I smiled grimly. "And do you know where she is now?"

"I wish I did. We had this argument, you see . . . well, not exactly an argument. She came round here early, seemed very worked up, then started asking me if I loved her and how much did I love her."

Inside my head I made yucking noises.

"Then I was just answering her as calmly as I could when she went crazy and stormed off. I never said a word to her," he protested.

"No, but you probably thought something," I muttered.

"What?"

"Never mind."

"Will you tell her I'm sorry for whatever it is I've done?"

"I might," I replied. Then seeing his stricken face, "I will, though personally I think you're better off without her."

So I knew she'd called at Tony's and used the crystal. But where was she now?

Then suddenly it didn't matter any

more. For staring up at me was the crystal. It was sitting on the path right by Tony's bin. Alison must have been so angry she'd flung it in there. How lucky she was a terrible shot.

I was so pleased to have the crystal back. I clipped it back on my belt loop. I'd never take it off – and I'd put an alarm on it.

Then I became angry. My sister had no business nicking my crystal like that and then just chucking it away as if it were an empty crisp packet.

I arrived back home.

"Ah good, you found your crystal," said Mum. "Where had you put it?"

"I hadn't put it anywhere," I muttered, through clenched teeth. "Is Alison back?"

"Yes, she came home in a terrible state, really upset about something. But she's sleeping now and I don't want her to be disturbed." Mum gave me a fierce look. "I'm sure you can sort out your little misunderstanding later."

Little misunderstanding. Thanks to Alison I could have lost for ever my most precious possession.

I hovered in the doorway of Alison's bedroom. "Alison, are you awake?" I hissed.

No reply.

I wanted to wake her up but I knew Mum would go crazy if I did that. Instead, I stood glaring at Alison, holding the crystal in my hand. "I got my crystal back, no thanks to you," I whispered. "You shouldn't have taken it."

There was a slight pause, then I "overheard" Alison reply: "I thought you'd tricked me somehow. I wanted to see if it really did work."

I stared at her in amazement. Alison was still asleep. But not only was she able to hear me, I could pick up her thoughts too. Or the crystal could.

"I wanted to see if Tony truly loved me," she went on, then she gave a little sob.

I stared at my sister in disgust. Fancy wasting the crystal on something as pathetic as that. I didn't feel sorry for her at all.

"Then I got so upset I threw it in the bin," she said.

"I know," I replied. The crystal got hot then, and while I was waiting for it to cool down I had a brainwave. I wasn't sure if it would work but it was worth a try.

After I'd tuned into Alison again I said, "Repeat after me – Matt's crystal hasn't really got any special powers."

"Matt's crystal hasn't really got any special powers," she chanted.

This was weird, amazing. For the first time in her life my sister was doing what I said.

"I imagined the whole thing," I continued.

"I imagined the whole thing," repeated Alison, in a dull, expressionless voice.

"Matt, what are you doing?"

I sprang round to see my mum frowning at me. "I told you not to disturb your sister. Now you can come and help me in the garden. Come on."

I didn't have time to check if my plan had worked. But if it had – well, that would be amazing. I could not only read minds, I could control them.

I felt suddenly flooded with power, even though I was picking up weeds at the time.

I wanted to go back and check on Bess. But Mum kept me busy all afternoon, while my sister slept on. It was after six o'clock when I finally escaped. I sped off to Miss West's house.

It was lucky I hadn't been any later, for a familiar figure was ahead of me. It was the bald-headed man I'd "overheard" plotting to kidnap Bess.

And he was walking up Miss West's drive.

Chapter Ten
Trapped

I RACED DOWN the street.

"Miss West, look out," I yelled.

The bald-headed man turned round.
I thought he was going to say
something to me. But instead he
hurried on.

And Miss West hadn't closed her door properly. Slap-head could just walk into her house. And that is what he did.

This was getting worse and worse. Right now he could be tying up poor Miss West and stealing Bess.

I pounded up the drive, dizzy with fear. The door was still open. I ventured inside. "Miss West, it's me, Matt. Are you all right?"

The house was eerily silent. No sign of Miss West. Or Bess either. That was most unusual. Bess usually rushes to the front door at the slightest sound.

I didn't like this at all. I moved inside a little further.

"Miss West, are you −" I began. Then

from nowhere something hit the top of my head. I heard someone cry out. A woman's voice — was it Miss West? The next moment I found myself falling . . . falling . . .

When I opened my eyes the room still seemed to be spinning. Where was I? I was lying on a bed. I scrambled to my feet, then immediately sagged back again. I staggered to the window. I recognized Miss West's back garden. Cally's football had an annoying habit of landing there. I was upstairs in a bedroom. I stumbled to the door. It wouldn't open. It was locked from the outside.

I half ran to the window again. It was locked too — and double glazed.

I was trapped inside here. I

wondered where Miss West was now. I shivered.

In the garden Bess was lying on the grass. But Slap-head was coming over to her, waving this meat in his hand. I worked out it had to be laced with some kind of sleeping pill. As soon as Bess had eaten it he could carry her away.

Bess was edging nearer the meat now. I guess the smell was irresistible.

Thick hedges grew on either side of the garden. No one else could see what was going on. Only me.

I had to do something.

I rattled on the window. I called out. But the glass was thick and all Bess's interest was on the meat. She was sniffing it now.

In a moment I'd have to watch Bess fall to the ground and that man creep away with her. I'd probably never see Bess again. She could be sold to someone thousands of miles away.

My eyes blurred.

I twisted my crystal around in frustration. Inside my head I screamed, "Bess, that meat is bad. You mustn't eat it. Do you understand? It's bad."

I let go of the crystal. At the same moment Bess stopped and turned her head on one side. She always does that when she's puzzled. It was just as if she'd heard me. But that was impossible. I'd tested the crystal on Bess and hadn't picked up anything.

But, boil my brains, I hadn't thought of the other possibility. What if Bess could hear *my* thoughts? After all, dogs do hear many sounds which we can't.

I grabbed the crystal again and waited for it to become warm. The next few seconds lasted for ever.

Then I saw Bess pick up the poisoned meat. My heart stopped. She flopped down on the grass, all set for a good feed. I held the crystal even tighter. It must be warm enough now. Then I sent this urgent message to Bess: "Drop the meat. It's not good for you. Drop the meat."

Again she cocked her head to one side. She could hear me all right. But she wasn't very keen to obey me.

Cally and I were always telling her to drop things she found in the garden. She had a special fondness for forget-me-nots, even though they always made her sick. When she didn't want to drop something Bess would lower her head and grip whatever it was more tightly. She was doing it now.

"Bess, drop it! Drop it now." Inside my head I was shouting at the top of my voice. My lips started moving too – even though no sound came out of them.

All at once Bess did drop the meat and then she began wagging her tail as if to say, "Haven't I been a good girl."

Slap-head bent down beside her. I guessed he was talking to her, urging Bess to pick the meat up again.

The crystal had become scorching hot. My whole body screamed with the pain. But I daren't let go of it now.

"Well done, Bess, now run away from the man. Run away."

Bess obeyed this instruction at once. I don't think she cared much for Slap-head anyway. She started bounding about the garden.

"Good girl, keep running. Don't let him catch you," I urged.

We sometimes played "He" with Bess and it was a game she loved. Perhaps she thought she was playing it now as she went leaping through the flower beds.

Then she stopped and looked around her as if she was trying to work out where I was hiding. Slap-head didn't try and follow her. He just stared at her in bewilderment.

He must have thought Bess had

gone mad. He picked up the meat and began calling to her again. But she just hid behind the tree for a moment, then started racing all around the garden again.

The crystal slipped from my fingers. I couldn't hold it any longer. My hands were as red as raw beef and they felt as if they were covered in wasp stings.

But what did that matter? Bess was safe – for now anyhow. And actually my fingers seemed to recover remarkably quickly.

The doorbell rang. The ringing vibrated through the whole house. I sprang to the bedroom door and yelled, "Help! Help! Help!"

I've never shouted so loudly in my life. But in reply, just a deafening silence. They must have gone away, whoever they were. I banged on the door in frustration.

Suddenly I froze. I could hear another sound: a clicking noise. I recognized it too. It was the sound of Miss West's back gate. The next moment I saw Cally and her parents walking into the back garden.

I rubbed my eyes. I wasn't hallucinating, was I? Slap-head looked pretty amazed too. He dropped the meat and stood as still as a marble statue. Bess raced over to Cally and her parents, madly excited to see them. Then she began tearing around the garden again. She was determined to play "He" with someone today.

Slap-head was talking to Cally's

mum and dad. I wondered what lies he was telling them. But Cally's parents looked suspicious. I guessed they were asking where Miss West was.

Meanwhile I was pounding furiously at the window. Finally Cally looked up – and saw me.

Chapter Eleven
Another Shock

"IT WAS JUST so lucky Bess didn't eat the meat," said Cally. "Do you suppose she knew it was poisoned?"

"I reckon she did." I patted her head. "She's a very good dog." I looked at Cally. "It was lucky you turned up when you did as well."

"Well, all day I was thinking about what you said and I didn't think you'd make that up, not about Bess. And then some of your other predictions have come true," said Cally. "So I pretended my tummy bug had come back. How do you feel now?"

"Oh, I'm fine," I said at once. It had been twenty minutes since I'd been let out of the bedroom and actually I still felt a bit shaky. Miss West had also been tied up and was very agitated. She sat drinking a cup of weak tea, while Cally's parents were interrogating Slap-head. They had already phoned the police.

He wasn't saying much, although I could see little purple veins pulsing on his head. In a low, dry voice he told how he'd just happened to spy Bess and thought he could get a good price for her. But somehow his story didn't seem quite right – not to me anyway.

"How did you know we would be away?" asked Cally's mum.

"I overheard you talking," he replied.

Then the police arrived. So Cally's parents and Slap-head left, while Cally and I stayed behind to comfort Miss West.

We sat chatting about what had happened and half by accident, I tuned into Miss West. I picked up something truly amazing. "This was such a mistake. I should never have let him talk me into this. Why do I always listen to my brother?"

Slap-head was her brother!

Did that mean Miss West was in on the plot too? Surely not, Miss West was nice – and she had a blue rinse, for goodness' sake. It was very hard to believe, or prove.

Then I had a brainwave. In the corner on the wall were some old black and white photographs. I got up and studied them carefully. Surely if Slap-head was her brother he'd be in one of these snaps. It took a while but I found one. He had a full head of hair then.

I nodded to Cally to come over. Looking a bit puzzled, she got up. I pointed at the photograph. "Who does that remind you of?"

Cally saw it at once. She rounded on

Miss West. "That man who was here, you know him. He's a relation of yours, isn't he? You're both in this together."

All the colour left Miss West's face. "My photographs," she whispered. "We never thought of that." Then she admitted Slap-head was indeed her brother.

"What were you going to do to Bess?" asked Cally. "Kidnap her and make us pay a ransom, or maybe you were going to kill her?"

"No, no," cried Miss West. "You mustn't believe that."

"I'd believe anything of you now," said Cally bitterly.

"You must let me tell you the truth," begged Miss West. The truth was this:

her brother was a dog breeder and he seemed all set to win a major prize with one of his dogs next month. He'd never won such an important prize before. There was only one obstacle: Bess. So the plan was to make it look as if Bess had been kidnapped when Miss West was looking after her.

"But honestly, truly," cried Miss West, "she'd have been safe with my brother's other dogs, and well looked after too. And as soon as the competition was over she'd have been returned to you, safe and very well."

"Thanks so much," murmured Cally with undisguised sarcasm. "Just for a stupid prize you'd inflict harm on an innocent dog, give me and my family a good deal of worry and hit Matt over the head."

"That wasn't meant to happen," said Miss West. Her shoulders sank lower and lower. "It's just when Matt turned up so suddenly, my brother over-reacted." She turned to me. "How did you know?"

"I saw your brother hanging around looking suspicious, that's all," I said. "And I got this bad feeling."

"Thank goodness you did," said Cally.

The phone rang. Miss West answered. "That was the police station," she said. "They want me to go too." She shook her head. I couldn't help feeling the tiniest bit sorry for her.

"Your mum and dad are on the way back," she said to Cally. "I'll just go and get ready."

"Shall we leave?" I asked Cally.

"No, I want to make sure she really goes to the police station," said Cally. She faced me. "If it hadn't been for you, poor Bess would have . . ." She shuddered. "Thank you, Matt."

I shrugged my shoulders. "All part of the service."

She went on, "I'd think you were a psychic person if it weren't for one thing."

"What's that?"

"How could you ever think I'd give my other Spurs ticket to Craig?"

"You would never believe me," I murmured.

"Well, you got some wrong information there," said Cally.

"You did go round Craig's house," I said suddenly.

"I was just being nosy," she replied. "But I didn't stay long. I always meant for you to have the other ticket, Matt. I was only teasing you. But it all went wrong. And, besides, you changed so much."

I looked at her curiously. "I did?"

"Oh yes. You never seemed to listen to me any more. You were always far away." Her voice rose. "It was horrible, it was like you'd been bewitched. You just weren't yourself."

"Well, I'm back now."

"About time," said Cally. Then she added, "The Spurs versus Arsenal match wasn't so great." A little smile crossed her face. "I think next Saturday's match will be much better."

Then I had to go to the doctor's for a check-up even though I said I felt fine.

Before I left, Miss West came downstairs to say goodbye. She apologized to both of us again. She even bent down and whispered, "Sorry" to Bess. She looked terrible; like a ghost.

She suddenly turned back to me and said, "That crystal you're wearing, Matthew. Excuse me for asking, but it reminds me so very much of a crystal a friend of mine wore. I always admired it so. Her name was Mrs Jameson."

That gave me a start.

"It is Mrs Jameson's," I said slowly. "She left it to me in her will."

"Well, fancy that. She and I worked together for nearly six years, you know. We were both secretaries, only she was much better than me. I could never read my shorthand back, she was always having to help me. It was such a shock when she left, and so suddenly too. Just marched out one day . . ."

It was then an idea sneaked into my head.

An amazing idea.

Chapter Twelve

Mind Reader Boy

I HAD TO wait until Monday before I could test it out.

I was bursting with impatience.

But after school I tore into the library. I stayed there until the library closed at six o'clock. I knew my mum would be cross but I couldn't move until I'd read every word of Mrs Jameson's message.

For at last I'd cracked the code and I'm sure you've guessed it as well. Mrs Jameson had ended her message to me in shorthand. Armed with a shorthand dictionary, I decoded: "Time is short and this is top secret but I know you will break my code easily."

I felt a real mouse-brain when I read that. The message continued: "I must tell you that my crystal has never brought me any happiness. I used it on the man I loved, my friends at work, and ended up a very sad, lonely woman. That is why I hesitate to give the crystal to you. Yet I know, if used wisely, it can be wonderful too. I think you are the one to discover its power for good. Goodbye.

Your friend,
Margaret Jameson.

P.S. There was only one person I never used the crystal on – and that was *you*, Matt."

I read her words over and over until I knew them by heart. Mrs Jameson's secret message to me.

She said the crystal lost her all her friends. Well, it nearly lost me my friendship with Cally. And my sister almost broke up with her boyfriend.

Did I tell you my sister apologized to me? Earth-shattering or what? It was after I got home on Saturday night. She told me she'd thought my crystal could read minds.

"But Matt's crystal hasn't really got any special powers, I'd imagined the whole thing." Her exact words. So I really had hypnotized her when she was asleep.

That should have made me feel very happy.

After all, I could hypnotize my sister again. She would have to obey my every thought. It sounded good at first. But I didn't want to turn anyone into my puppet, not even Alison. That would be seriously spooky.

So was Mrs Jameson's letter.

She was telling me the crystal had turned her into a kind of freak.

And the same could happen to me.

That's why I put the crystal away in my cupboard. And that's where it stayed for a whole ten minutes.

Then I saw Cally coming along the road with Bess. They were calling for me. Cally looked so happy. But if it hadn't been for my crystal . . . well, Bess would be far away now.

I took the crystal out of the cupboard again.

I decided I couldn't keep it hidden away. What a waste. But I'd make up some new rules.

Rule One: never use it on my family and friends.

Would you believe, I've kept that rule for one whole week.

Not that I haven't been tempted. You see, it's my birthday next month and

I'm mad keen to know what my mum's bought me.

My hand's certainly twitched a few times.

But I was strong.

From now on I'll only use my crystal for good things, like solving mysteries.

For with great power goes great responsibility – as Spiderman once said.

And what's good enough for Spiderman is good enough for Mind Reader Boy.

Don't worry, I'm not really going to call myself that. But if I can ever help you, remember there's no need to write or phone – just send a few thoughts my way.

I'll be listening.